# FROM THE HEART

A Collection of

Short Stories

Copyright © 2016 Jamie Henshaw

All rights reserved. No part of this collection may be used or reproduced in any manner whatsoever without written permission from the author.

For information regarding permission, please visit WWW.WordsBecomeMe.Weebly.com.

ISBN-10:1539968251
ISBN-13: 978-1539968252

For you.

-The Heart

# CONTENTS

Acknowledgments

| | |
|---|---|
| Glasses | 1 |
| Hearts | 23 |
| Ashes | 34 |
| Guide Dog | 40 |
| Immortal | 54 |
| Phonograph | 62 |
| King Najra | 69 |
| The Tree in Concord Park | 73 |
| Firebox | 82 |
| The Words of Another | 107 |

# ACKNOWLEDGMENTS

Jen, my wife, my greatest encouragement, and my pillar of support. This wouldn't be here without you. And I wouldn't be *here* without you. Thank you for everything you are and everything you do.

Coryn, my dear bookworm, whose love of reading makes me want to keep creating. You are inspiring, and you lift my spirits high. Thank you for sharing this part of me.

Katharine, my friend and forger of words. You helped me find my thoughts many times. A couple of these came from our prompts. Thank you for helping me find words.

Tim & Carol, my parents, for your story telling (still don't know what happened in that ice rink), and love of words (I look up every one I don't know). Thank you for these passions.

And many readers who have offered insight and ideas that helped bring these stories to life including: Meriona, Cookie, Lauri, Jim, Brenda, Jerry, Jo, Lizz, Anthony, Matt, Jen, Kelsey, Joanna, Katy, Mary, Theresa, Laurie… and on and on the list goes. Thank you.

# GLASSES

"Yes – sir. We have coffee and sandwiches. This is a bistro."

Old people. I mean, really old people. We say things like, "poor fella, his mind is slipping" when, in fact, he's driving you BAT-SHIT-CRAZY!

After his wife repeated my words, "They have coffee and sandwiches!" - yelling into his left ear two more times, he said, "Oooh," and then mispronounced the word 'bistro'. He ordered the Tuscan Soup.

It's a good job, don't get me wrong. Employees get discounts on the plethora of tasty food options. There's outdoor serving in the warm weather, cozy indoor heating during the cold seasons. And there are always plenty of new faces all the time on account of the business around the corner. A business cram-packed with old people shopping for old things; old people whose minds are slipping, if you catch my drift.

They're always telling me their names and showing kindness and a hospitable nature that gives them away as not being from around here. Not to say everybody here is awful; just that the uber-kindness of the visiting elderly sets them apart. The old man who ordered Tuscan Soup at table 3 kept calling me Jonas and asking me when I'd go back to college. "Soon as I get back on my own two feet," I told him. See I've dealt with oddities like that before and have a special way of handling them. It helps them cope with the changing world. It puts a smile on their face, gives them resolve where they might not have it. Plus when they come with a sane spouse or friend I get an extra big tip for being so understanding and nice.

I could always tell if they were coming from or going to that warehouse looking place that brought them all around. There was a certain heavy smell of aged dust that clung to their jackets and sweaters. It also gave away the less aged that went there, typically beanie wearing hippies from campus who wanted their dorms to be more "eclectic". Aside from the smell the place left on them, it was pretty common to see an item or two from their haul as it sat on their table while they looked it over, serving as conversation pieces until they brought it home to their own heap of stuff. Vases that possibly had something to do with a Dynasty, wooden boxes with hidden latches or missing keys, any metallic object you could think of – only with rust on the edges.

It wasn't the trinkets that kept them going on with life, and it wasn't the trinkets that kept them coming. It was probably something along the lines of the mystery of life which seemed embodied in the things they bought; things they probably overpaid for. Unless, of course, the sellers were in the same mental state as the wandering customers, in which case things were probably sold at a fraction of their worth. For a year I worked at the bistro before ever actually going into that place.

# GLASSES

It was actually en route between my house and work, except that I usually skipped the streets in favor of the alleyways. You might understand – that there comes a point where you just don't want to be around people anymore. But, I was feeling sociable that day, felt like I could handle a little more bat-shit-crazy, and like my twenty dollar tip for being "Jonas" was burning a hole in my pocket.

When my shift ended I took the streets home and found myself window shopping at the Emporium. The name made it sound a little bit more grand than it actually seemed. And what it still is I imagine, a place like that doesn't fold up or shut down. There will always be old things for people to have an interest in. The very things in our homes today will end up there, eventually. But "what's in a name?" or "a rose by any other name" or something like that.

Evening was setting in, those few moments when shadows are cast in the most appealing ways which photographers always go scampering about trying to capture. An angel in the cemetery, black post fences, trees beginning to crisp and lose their leaves, things of that nature. The store was set in such a way that the sun streamed through the large windows on either side of the entrance so that some of the more interesting objects on display cast long shadows that would keep a child awake at night.

My reflection stared back at me in the left side bay window, a dying sunlight on my back. I'm not as average as a yawn; maybe a sigh, or a shrug. Hair color somewhere between dark blond and brown. 5 foot 10, not particularly muscular, but not terribly thin. And at least, as I usually compare against the rest of my family, no need for contacts or glasses.

That's the important thing, no glasses. The only glasses I've ever worn were made for the sun. My favorite pair, long since lost, was a pair of "blue blockers", yellow lenses that tone down the blue of the sky but do little for any of the more direct sunlight. Somehow I always seemed to have my back to the sun anyway.

# GLASSES

I hadn't expected anything in particular when I walked in, but when I didn't hear the jingling of tiny bells hitting the door as it opened, it caught my attention. Strange how sometimes things aren't apparent until they aren't there. The word "Welcome" wasn't on the mat, two of the cash registers weren't staffed, and the third table of wares I looked at was missing a large vase. (I could tell by the faint lack-of-dust mark between two other vases. Which also meant it had been recently bought.)

I did, however, find several pieces of jewelry I might have fancied were I a woman, an old hand carved chess board, and a tarnished pocket watch with an elaborate series of intricate concentric circles with long straight lines and sporadic dots. From somewhere in the back a long and mournful song full of memory was being played on an ill-tuned piano. Slow, slower than a dance, the notes flowed between artifacts, surrounding everything. I never went to see who was playing, a choice I don't regret. The ambiguity of not knowing who played that music lets me wonder, even to this day, if I'm looking that man or woman in the face while serving coffee at the bistro. It could be anyone at all; in a way, it would be everyone.

Most every booth is owned by a different person, and most every person was old and retired having little else to do but sell off their remaining belongings. The wares set out in front of each and every one of them would have a clean slate in the possession of a new owner, losing nearly all of their worth when the memory was separated from the object. For this reason, if you don't leave the booth quickly enough, you're likely to hear the full history of whatever you decide to (or not to) purchase.

I don't go there anymore. Thinking about how all those objects would be robbed of their memories when purchased (very much like the aging sellers would be robbed of their memories as time took them in one by one) brings me a sadness that is too difficult to face. I have been filled with the urge to know about everything there. But there simply isn't enough time to learn about them all, and I can't decide which stories to

## GLASSES

hear and which ones to leave to their inevitable demise.

One booth in particular, owned by a woman whose nametag bore the name Mildred, held such an assortment of wares, as opposed to others which seemed to reflect collecting a particular sort of item, I couldn't help but take a closer look. Edison rolls for an old phonograph, their song titles faded with sun decay and time. More jewelry and watches, all of which were underpriced and ripe for the investing. A stamp collection that even my untrained eyes knew was a good find. A pair of glasses, of the faintest prescription, wire rimmed, and held by tape around the middle. I picked up the glasses. Of all the things my eyes had settled on in the half hour of wandering, it was the only thing I touched. And to think, it was probably the lack of interest that compelled me to it.

Even for wire rimmed glasses made of real glass, where today we use plastics of one sort or another, they were remarkably light. She sat in her chair knitting, glancing around the room periodically, keeping track of her friends (or co-workers, in some fashion). I was looking at the glasses, carefully turning them in my hand as though I was in a museum and the curator allowed me to remove them from a case, when she broke into sudden conversation.

"Those belonged to my late husband. My second husband, that is. Wonderful soul he was, let me tell you. Never much had two dimes to rub together, he and I, but if we had – he'd have given them to a perfect stranger if he thought it would help them half as much as it would help him." Something about her voice rang with an English accent. She had a light pink blouse, thoroughly grayed hair, and a pair of more-modern glasses of her own perched rather low on her nose, and her hands never stopped their learned knitting.

She had gone from the glasses, to her husband, to the hard times, in a matter of seconds. I pressed on about the item, "These must have cost quite a bit back in the day?"

## GLASSES

"Oh, back in the day, you say. Back in the day." She set down her needles on her lap. I had the sense that the recollection of her late husband was merely a common speech she made, and that now she was beginning to lose herself to actual thought. "Oh, days long past always seem to hold the most wonderful memories, don't you think? The farther away you get from hard times the less you remember about the struggle and the more you remember the good times. You know, I almost can't remember what it was like to be in such hard times as those. Might as well have been nothing but good times, after all these years. Despite the difficulty of stretching a dollar for groceries, or mending the same clothes for some eight years; and it was a long stretch of luck and a good job that he was able to manage even those things. Good times, I call that." My redirection hadn't worked the way I expected. She seemed happier to just twitter on, so I let her – the weightlessness of the wire-framed and held by tape glasses all but forgotten in my hands.

"They were hard times though?" I asked,

with more interest and curiosity than I knew was there.

"Oh, they were hard times, sure enough. But if you've got time for a good cry, a moment for a heavy sigh, or a few seconds for a kiss from someone that loves you – no times are too hard." Her nostalgia consumed her, more positive moments I assumed. I let her have them, staying still and quiet. I'd have appreciated that if I was her.

Mildred smiled at me after a few moments and went on knitting some patterned thing that I can't begin to describe other than the single word "elegant". I asked her how much for the glasses. She looked at them, seeing them on his face, seeing the memories flash by and wondering if she could bear to risk forgetting. When you spend so much effort moving past hard times and clinging to the good ones, the worst fear in the world is losing the memories you've kept. A loss like that doesn't leave behind a faint dust ring, though. It's simply gone like it was never there, like it never happened. One less good moment, one less refreshing sigh, one less kiss from someone that loves you…

"Oh, I don't know, deary. What do *you* think is fair? Five dollars?"

I smiled and reached for the twenty in my pocket. I offered her the whole of it. Not because I wanted to patronize Mildred, or because I felt bad for her. He would have spared his change, simple as that. If she ever forgot him, maybe she would remember the stranger that had a similar notion.

When she saw it she shook her head at my offering, smiling wide. "Up at the front if you don't mind, young man. They try very hard to keep track of their books here. But rest assured, I'll get it." I acknowledged the tiny tag on an earpiece designated for her booth. "And thank you." She paused, focusing on my face, perhaps trying her best to memorize it. "He would be glad to know this is how it happened."

Bat shit crazy, I expected. But she was sweet,

and kind. I hope that I remain kind when today becomes the "good old days". A couple more friendly smiles later and I headed for the cash register in the front. There were a few people in line ahead of me; one of those beanie-wearing hippies, and (not surprisingly) more old people.

The cashier was properly accustomed to the array of people that wandered in and out. She was used to the molasses speed in which the majority of the customers fussed with pocket books and well-worn leather wallets. She wasn't wearing a name tag, and no name I thought of seemed good enough to be hers. She seemed to have come from a different world. Like if Dorothy had started out in Oz and landed in the black and white world. But more than that, she looked like brilliance and creativity waiting only for the end of the day when the fresh air and freedom of the outside world would take its place with her again.

I hope I wasn't staring because I didn't realize it was my turn to pay until someone nudged me. I carefully set my minute haul on the

## GLASSES

table; another late realization, that I hadn't continued to peruse the wares after finding the wire-rimmed glasses. I'm not sure if it was actually my intent to buy anything while I was there, but it wasn't my intent at that moment to leave without more. For fear of looking even more ridiculous than I had already allowed myself to be, I simply went along with it.

"Just the glasses here," I mumbled less audibly than was polite, and I was sorry for that. I set the money on the table.

She looked at me, she didn't really seem to have looked much at the customers in front of me, and simply said, "Nothing here is *just*". Without asking how I wanted to take my glasses home, she was packing them up in a brown bag with some foam stuff. I almost told her not to bother because they were already broken. Instead I watched as the glasses were handled with caution and care. It might well have been her own treasure being sold off. She handed me the bag and smiled.

## FROM THE HEART

It took a bit of effort not to look back when I left the place. To not look back at Mildred, to not look back at the other tables, to not look at the cashier. After crossing the street, the urge grabbed hold of me to wear them. Never having a need for wearing glasses, I didn't know if they would look good on me or not. I hadn't imagined actually wearing them when I bought them. I took them out and studied the break at the nose. They didn't seem as fragile as they might have been, and setting them to my face, I found them to be quite comfortable. They might as well have been made for me.

Meaning to look at myself in the large office building windows in front of me, my attention was instead drawn to the reflection of the place I bought them. The Emporium. I had never before looked at the place properly, with the kind of open eyes that are willing to see the world for what it really is. Like Mildred's second husband. I never even asked his name, but I wanted to look at the world through his eyes. So I turned away from the backward, mirrored world to face it in all its truth.

Then there was glowing all around me. It seemed they were worse off than a break in the nosepiece. I had to flip the glasses up from my eyes several times to understand what I was seeing. The people in the streets were glowing! My bare eyes could see dozens of pedestrians, but through the glasses their forms vanished and were replaced by the likes of deep purples and bright oranges, reflecting off of everything.

A man walking his dog was glowing yellow with wisps of teal, a woman coming out of a coffee shop glowed green, and so on. Finally it came to me, when I saw a couple holding hands and whispering; both of them shared a twirling arrangement of orange, red, and pink. They were in love, and they were the colors of love. As people continued to walk by, in the cooling shades of evening, a mighty aura filled the street.

I couldn't resist a long walk, looking as much into people as at them, flipping the glasses up and down on my face, realizing slowly that it was completely obvious what color each person would glow with. Their faces, the way they walked, it was all very telling. I had simply never taken the time to notice before.

Instead of taking the glasses off when my eyes began to feel tired from the glow, I took a few back alleyways away from the main streets and people. On a sort of auto-pilot, my legs took me back to the bistro where I worked instead of home. Old people were sitting here and there with the inevitable wares and trinkets of the day. Colors of contentment and joy were at all of their tables. I could even swear faint colors seeped from their purchases at The Emporium.

It occurred to me at once what I had been neglecting to see, to look at, and I rushed past everybody to the back of the bistro, to the bathroom. With the glasses flipped up I checked the room to make sure I was quite alone. Anybody would think I was nuts for what I was about to do.

I stood square in front of the mirror and took

## GLASSES

a deep breath, hands poised and ready to wear those magic glasses held by tape. With my eyes closed, I slid them onto my nose and my heart raced with all manner of wonder and curiosity. For what colors might be there? What hopes and dreams do I call mine? And when I opened my eyes I realized it was the one thing nobody could be prepared to see. For an eternity my feet held me stock still, hoping against all hope that they simply didn't work on the wearer. What was there - I saw those magic glasses held in empty space.

I took them back immediately.

The same girl was at the counter, two registers still unstaffed. I hoped that Mildred wouldn't see me in the line again returning the glasses from her late husband who was such a giver and a great man. He must have loved seeing the colors of his wife and he must have had the most amazing colors to look at in the mirror. Even if she had a bad memory, it hadn't been more than an hour since I was there and she would easily recognize and remember me.

## FROM THE HEART

The line moved much slower than it did before. The idea crept into my mind to actually keep them, to try again or to ignore my lack of color and enjoy what everybody else had – perhaps give myself something to aspire to. But then it was my turn at the register.

"Back so soon?" She raised an eyebrow. "This place does that to you. What will it be this time?" The woman with no name tag thought I was buying something else.

"I-I'm returning. These. The glasses. I'm returning these glasses." I'm an idiot.

She looked puzzled, "Really? I thought they'd look good on you. Can I see?"

I offered her the glasses, still holding them carefully. They'd be valuable to somebody, I was sure. Somebody with more substance and care and love for the world. Not some guy who works at the bistro. Who thinks all the old people that have come to The Emporium to be little more than crazy and senile and generally on their way out. Who judges the beanie-wearing hippies and rolls his eyes when they order cappuccino and biscotti.

"No, I mean you – wearing them. Put them on, dear." Lots of people use words like "dear" and "love" and "hon" when they're talking to people. It never particularly catches my attention, but my heart skipped half a beat when she used it – even though she was simply talking to just another a person. Just another person… Nothing here is just, she had said.

I fidgeted awkwardly, not wanting to put them back on. As long, I figured, as I wasn't going to see myself again. They went to my face and she was gone, as the magic goes. Only she wasn't gone the same way I was. Where she had been were bright oranges and yellows, vibrant reds and organic greens, there were colors I don't have words for nor has the world perhaps seen - and breathing didn't work anymore.

"Yeah, I think they're very you. I know a guy who can fix them for you if you want. He owes me for a deal I got him here last week, wouldn't cost you a penny." I was still staring at the colors of her, spinning over each other as she spoke. I recognized a few of the colors from the people in the streets. Happiness was there, joy, and contentment with probably everything in her life.

"You think so?" I managed to say, and her colors swirled. "Um… I guess. Yeah. That'd – that'd be great, actually."

Colors shifted to the fore-front within her, ones I recognized from my walk but wasn't making much sense of at the moment. I caught a glimpse of the floating glasses in the reflection of a small mirror that was standing on the counter with a tiny tag hanging from it; another item for sale that went almost unnoticed.

She asked me to meet her after her shift that evening at eight. I was never busy in the evenings, so I agreed to. Within the mirror came a faint swirl, similar to what she glowed with and my first thought was that her brilliance was shining off my glasses. A reflection of a

## GLASSES

reflection. But no. What I saw was the start of colors in me. And our colors were beginning to match. Like the couple holding hands I'd seen earlier…

# HEARTS

When the door closed, and the draft from the cruel cold of the outside world subsided, she was standing there, still as a statue, trying to decide whether or not to stay.  Most people come in with purpose; it was unusual to see such hesitation.  Things were slow and I wouldn't have noticed otherwise.  Business is busy this time of the year for the most part, what with seasonal depression and all.  But this one didn't seem to want to admit she needed a drink.

Frankly I was sort of glad.  I mean, I have a talent for knowing the right drink to pour.  When folks come in asking for something and I can tell it's the wrong one, I almost feel offended that they didn't ask for my advice.  You go out to buy a new appliance, you ask for advice.  You go to buy furniture, you ask for advice.  It's my bar and I know what's best for you.  Otherwise, why

## HEARTS

didn't you just stay at home?

She was wearing a short black skirt, stood up straight, and was just a little on the tall side. I'm sure she didn't like being stared at the way I was, but it wasn't for her looks. I was figuring her out. Her long sleeved white shirt seemed just a little on the crumpled side, she hadn't changed to go out – she probably hadn't gone home yet.

My staring didn't go unnoticed, though it must have at least been more study than gawk because she decided to stay and sit at the bar, right next to a regular. It struck me, when she was right next to this other fella, that not only was her white shirt a little bit more white - her sleeves were more cluttered.

"What would you like?" I asked her, allowing her the kindness of making the choice. I wished I'd been doing something clever like drying a cup, or making another drink. Instead, my hands were perched on my hips, trying to casually look at the words wrapping around her sleeves. She shrugged.

## FROM THE HEART

I held up a finger for a moment's pause, glad to be allowed to do what I do best. Turning away to conceal the labels, I went about mixing from a few bottles into a glass cup, filling it no more than halfway. Take it easy on the newcomers; that's how I always keep it. "Here you go. See if that helps you any."

The door drifted open again. Mister "half-and-half" stumbled in and pushed the door shut behind him. The guy really needed to see about getting himself a different shirt; spots were so soiled that they would likely never come clean no matter what he did. I had his cup, near full to the brim, ready as he got to the bar and he took it up as he sat down. Half-and-Half nodded his head curtly and began to drink. It's not good for anybody to focus so much like he does. Different strokes for different blokes, the saying goes, I guess; moreover, I guess the saying meant him.

It isn't a habit of mine to ask names; I never did get hers, but she was one of the few I wished I'd asked. At any rate, the new girl had taken several sips by the time I had turned back around

## HEARTS

to her side of the bar. The look on her face was telling, the flavor had struck a chord with her. "What exactly is this?" she asked me in as polite an inquiry as she could.

"Special blend, just for you." It didn't answer her question, so I continued. "Well, in terms of the drink: a little bit of grief, a little solitude, and a dash of could-have-been."

Still, she wasn't getting the idea of it, and drank some more to figure it out on her own. The blank expression she had walked in with was changing, as it does, while the new emotions seeped into her veins. The week had been rough for her, that much I could tell by her shirt, and like everybody else she had come in to process it. Another glass of the stuff would have likely torn her into a handful of pieces. So, when she asked for a second without specifying the same, I mixed a different blend for her.

Half-and-half at the other counter had already finished his blend; he drinks too fast. His brow was furrowed and the edges of his lips turned down. The usual reaction to the usual drink. I'd given up asking him if I could choose his second drink, and he signaled me for another. I may disagree, but it's my job to serve what I'm asked for. Loss and grief; 50/50. It isn't good for anybody to delve too deep like he does. He wiped his face with the edge of his shirtsleeve; not smudging the ink, but dirtying the cuff yet another shade away from white.

The girl took only a sip to start, like I had told her to, and she immediately changed, almost crying. As indiscreetly as possible, I watched her sleeves to see if anything would change. Nothing. Maybe after she finished.

I stood square in front of her, placed my hands on the bar and waited for her eyes to meet mine. The black of my bar shirt stood sharply in contrast to her own whites, and the whites of the gentleman sitting next to her, who had barely touched his drink for twenty minutes. It's my job alone that allows a person to wear that; a not-white shirt. Customers would get distracted if they could see the words on my sleeves. That was

# HEARTS

an early lesson in my career. I've got my own things to deal with. And I sure can't stand around sneaking sips, the last thing these people want is an emotional bar keep. As for my drinks of choice, just between you and me, I like the first glass to be solitude, regret, and sadness, and the second to be friendship, acceptance, and a healthy portion of happiness. After hours, of course.

"Value," I kindly explained to the woman. "Confidence. Mostly self-worth. Thought you could use it." At last she looked at me, realizing only then that it was exactly how she was feeling. "It's a talent of mine. Pouring the right drink, the right feelings…" Her eyes turned back to her glass. "I've never seen you here before. You a customer looking for a new place to soften the world, or is this your first time in a bar?"

I think she took it much more personally than I intended to. I busied myself with drying an already dry cup and tried to forget the question. The man next to her, who was clearly a world away, finally took his glass and downed the whole thing in a single mouthful. Dammit. I'd have to keep an eye on him for that move. Don't ever do that.

"This," the girl said and pointed to a particular word on her sleeve, "this has been there for as long as I can remember." She made a sound like a half-hearted chuckle through her nose. "Might as well be tattooed on my skin." INVALUE. Probably not a real word, but it's interpretive, it's what was inside.

"What'll you do when it's gone?" It was most definitely an intrusive question, but the shot of self-worth was doing its job and she took the question in stride. Her only response, however, was to shake her head slowly; almost worried to imagine its impossible absence.

"What about you then?" she asked. "Do you stand around and drink all day? I mean, you seem like you genuinely want to help. But it's not exactly a normal thing without a glass of Help or something in your hand, is it?" This was not the same hesitant woman who had walked in some time ago, and her thoughts were beginning to

# HEARTS

flow. Obviously enjoying the freedom of it, she drank a healthy sized gulp and looked straight at me.

I didn't exactly know how to answer that. It was my job, first and foremost. My place was to mix the drinks for people who needed them. Her job may well have been to file hundreds of forms for hundreds of clients; and really, the level of obligation seemed the same to me. Yet the question implied I also experienced a desire to help, or received a satisfaction from doing so. But no, I don't drink until after hours so… how could it be possible to experience those things? But then, my white shirt hanging in a locker in the back room clearly had the word PROCLAIM. I had to look it up to be sure why it was there. To declare something that one finds important. To show others. Imagine a word like that on your sleeve.

But it's only words without the drinks. And it's only a job. Serving drinks to bring out the words in the heart. If there was any real compulsion to do what's in me, well there must be something wrong with me – something broken.

"It's just a job." I managed to say. But her comment had caused damage to my thoughts, which rallied around the words she couldn't see on my bar keep's black sleeves. Genuine, patience, familiar, teacher, friend. And with my thoughts came a desire to feel those things at that moment. Somehow they all seemed positive in nature, and yet there I stood in a shirt that hid them from the world. A world that can't even see the words for their worth without a damned drink in their hands. "Broken" didn't seem like such a bad thing at that moment. If I could be those things without waiting for my turn after-hours…

"Yeah. Just a job." I smiled at her, trying to convince both of us that it was true. "What about you? What do you do?" I needed the focus to be on something not me. I was also curious.

She finished off her drink, not asking for more, and said, "funny you should ask. Actually I treat animals."

## HEARTS

"Animals? What in the world for?"

"Study. They seem to express something that I had never seen before. These cats and dogs, they seem to have missed me when I get to work in the mornings. They stand on the table next to me... sometimes even sit on my lap, look at me and purr or lick my face. There is quite a bit of studying being done to try and understand them, for reasons like that. Science is looking for a way to make them better." She spun her glass in circles, thinking it over. "I mean, they can't read. But somehow they almost seem to react to what's on... this is going to sound strange... what's on somebody's sleeves. Weird, right?"

"Yeah, weird."

"Funny thing, though..." I remained attentive for her to finish the thought, which took a moment or two to form and produce itself. "Now, two drinks in... it doesn't seem all that unusual." My attention remained hers alone, but she didn't say another word. She gently touched at that word on her sleeve, INVALUE. I could've sworn the word was darker than that when she came in. Then she simply pulled out a bit of money, set it on the counter, and walked through the doors for the second and final time.

After the draft from the cruel cold of the outside world subsided once again, I was left to attend to the small number of customers who still sat on their stools, with their drinks in their hands, and even occasionally drank. I took her glass and washed it, wiped it with a towel, and set it on the drying rack upside-down. A single drop slid down the side of the glass and fell to the counter; like a lone tear, or a leap of faith.

I'm not embarrassed by my white shirt, and I don't mean to hide behind that black one. Even on the dark material, I still know what words are where. Maybe I really do want to help. Maybe I am unusual, backwards, wrong, broken... And maybe, now I mean just maybe, I'm better at my job for it.

And maybe it's not just a job.

# ASHES

"Not a day goes by," they used to say, "When you are not in my heart." Before long business trips, after fights, and quiet evening toasts over candlelit dinners. It wasn't just a sweet thing they said when sharing a moment, but a promise for all others to come.

"Not a day goes by," was sometimes all they would say. The other words would echo in the heart and soul. They would hold hands or slow dance, and a hug could last an hour; the unspoken always heard. But somehow in the accident, amidst the panic and the tears, the words didn't come. Now that he was alone, the words couldn't come.

Along the top of an upright baby grand piano sat a row of carefully labeled jars, the smallest on the left and each one a little bigger. His hand rested for a moment on this small one while memories played of little Alex, with his black and white paws, swatting furry toys and dust bunnies, purring. The memory of Alex wound around his right ankle, wound around his left ankle, and twitched its tail against his leg.

Life is made of moments, and life is a moment. It's why we wear a watch, he thought, to remind ourselves that these moments are passing us by. We can never hold such an intangible thing in our hands; but if we don't try, we'll never hold onto anything. The row of jars and their contents could be nothing more than a representation of life, and a last chance to hold the something they were.

His hands touched the next two lids, sibling pups that had grown strong and knew loyalty. A treat was always left in front of Baxter's jar for the time he saved Gabriella, who fell into a small pit and couldn't get back out, staying with her and howling for help. Baxter, as his mind brought the image into being, padded into the living room and sniffed at this and that. Peter came too, quickly finding Alex cleaning his paws and gave chase across the house. A small smile couldn't be helped when Baxter sighed the way he always did and ambled after, ready to break up the games should they get out of hand.

The fourth container was different, decorated and important. It shined and caught the light in a way that was just so, but he did not touch it. No, not yet. Just another moment.

Instead he sat down on the piano bench and with movements that were well practiced and, in this moment, forced, fingers found their keys, like actors taking marks on the stage. Their choreography was to a lullaby that sounded to his heart both well-known and on the edge of forgotten. It sighed in the minors, and it smiled as it danced, and dreams, but for a moment, felt worth a chance. It was a song of hope and it was the only thing he had ever written, and he had written it for her.

When the last notes faded, when the ears had to admit the void that followed, he slowly reached a hand forward. Blindly he reached while his eyes clenched shut; closer to the shine that reflected the room, closer to the jar that held Gabriella, to that last chance to hold the something she was. A small hand touched him, as he found the cool of the object, and gently rubbed his back. Like the swaying motion of a tree or the sea, his daughter that wasn't there comforted him while his clenched eyes wept. A smile as pure as hers didn't need to be seen, and he wished he could clear his vision to catch it before she left. But he didn't. No, not yet.

The final jar he wasn't sure he could touch, tall and slender, like a vase with no flower. It was a dark and heavy grey, soft and warm as a metal can be. His eyes fell to the engraving that wrapped around the base, a promise for all moments to come. And he sat there, wishing he could say it.

Then she was there, stealing his breath away, sweeping into the room with an emptiness where always there had been joy. She came and stood beside him, she touched a few of the keys and breathed. She stared at the jars, seeing the ashes

# ASHES

for their loss. Her hand instinctively found the tallest, and her tears found release. She shook her head, rubbing the inscription with her fingers like a tender caress. But all the will in the world couldn't turn it into flesh.

He rose to his feet, chest shuddering, and held her. The warmth felt unlike a memory; it was real, and it taunted him. With all the strength he had in his being a whisper managed to pass his lips to her ears, and in his breath were the words "not a day goes by".

She fell hard to the floor, passing through his arms, sobbing and howling into the still air. She screamed at death, and she cursed at life. She held herself, oh so tightly, when nobody else could, and called out to him by name, but she didn't see him.

There was nothing he could do for her, and nothing he wouldn't do for her. Once again a small hand found him, holding his hand and swaying his arm like a tree, or like the sea. At his side he found the little girl who may well have been made of love. What a pure and beautiful smile.

# GUIDE DOG

My old man was the kind of guy that would sell you the watch off your right wrist by convincing you it would be improved on your left. He was charismatic and likeable. He was passionate and convincing. He was a bullshit artist that made a killing at a garage. If he wasn't trying to win you over, he was trying to win what he wanted.

This all coming from somebody who actually liked the guy; well, except for the time he convinced me to trade him the change in my piggy bank for the cash in his wallet because "paper money is better". I lost fifteen dollars to him that day and learned two valuable lessons: One – the value of a dollar. Two – not to get conned by what looks good at the time.

It might come as a surprise to you that I took a job in marketing getting paid to pull the same wool over everyone else's eyes. Only I did it with billboards and newspaper advertisements. Maybe I just came to figure that if you're not going to think for yourself and be careful with money, you've probably got enough thought and money to spare on what I'm selling you. Maybe I hoped to teach somebody else the same lesson I had learned as a child. Value.

I liked to watch commercials with Billy, a dog that I adopted, and laugh at the way they show pups turning up their noses at "The Other Brand" in favor of "The Very Best". It's just a marketing trick, you see. You don't even want to know what's actually in the "other" bowl, but be sure it's not food and there's no dog in the world that would eat it. Except maybe Billy; the poor guy was on his way out and it was all I could do to keep him comfortable. He didn't need the very best of anything, he only wanted to be happy.

Billy used to be a guide dog; probably the best and most noble of them all. He had pulled back on his harness one day and saved his owner's life. No that's not quite right, he saved his friend's life. An SUV had lost control and Billy put himself in the middle. At least that's the story I got from the man at the shelter. Billy caught my attention as soon as I walked in; he was mostly blind and walked with a limp, but when he saw me his tail wagged. He'd been through a lot and I just wanted to be the one to take care of him.

I noticed in those days that there is a distinct difference between what you do and what you DO. There was this job, this marketing thing that I was good at, and it paid the bills and it made for a comfortable life. And there was this dog, this remarkable being that needed care and attention. What I do, what I DO. Funny, how the answer would depend on who was asking "What do you do?" We measure success in different ways, but we respond based on how we think somebody else measures it.

I was called in to a business and marketing meeting for a toilet paper company one day. They wanted the same thing all corporate moguls want: to sell more of what they've got. Twenty men and women sitting around a table in an oversized conference room were discussing how to sell more toilet paper, what they can do to make toilet paper better, how to make toilet paper more appealing, and anything else you can think of as long as it was about toilet paper. I couldn't help laughing to myself just a little bit, but it was enough for the suit at the end of the table to notice.

"Are we wasting your time, young man?" he asked me, pointing an expensive ballpoint pen in my direction. I put my hand up apologetically but before I could respond he continued. "You're in the business of selling, right? Selling anything. And from what I've heard, you're pretty damn good at it. That's why you're here. Now Jones over there is a vegetarian, think you can sell him a steak?" Jones looked worried he was going to end up leaving with a suitcase of expensive steaks. "Erica, that pretty lady in the blazer, she's an AA member, think you could ask her out for a drink?" Erica was horrified, she avoided looking at me altogether.

"Maybe, but they're a tough sell," he said, "they don't even want those things." The suit put down his pen parallel to the leather bound notebook in front of him, and put his hands together with woven fingers. "There are few things that everybody in the world has in common, and one of them just happens to be about the grossest thing a person can do. Everybody shits, kid. And everybody," he waved his arm across the table, "has an ass to wipe. You don't have to pitch something like toilet paper 'cause everybody is going to buy it. The thing is, I want them to buy MY toilet paper." He leaned forward and lowered his voice. "How can I make them buy my toilet paper, kid?"

A few months later a lot more people were buying his toilet paper. Money for paper. Paper for paper. Anything can be sold, and anything can be bought. At least that's exactly what I thought until Billy took another turn for the worse. His breathing became labored, his eyes looked right through me, and I had to bring his food to him. I bought him the best food I could find; which, honestly, I think made me happier than it made him.

## FROM THE HEART

    While the money was still coming in for making some old product sound better, the money was going out trying to make Billy comfortable. Every idea the vet pitched to me was sold before they finished explaining it. Anything can be bought, I kept hoping. This can be bought, I kept thinking. But then came our last night together.

    I knew it was time. Like those last moments before a storm when the air cools and the wind rushes by in the leaves, and thunder rumbles in the distance. I hefted him up onto my bed, extra pillows, extra blankets, I even put his food and water dishes right there next to him. I rubbed along his nose and scratched behind his ears. I wished he had never been hurt. It would mean him not having saved that woman, and it would mean us never meeting. I even wished those things for just a moment. But Billy had such an amazing life in him, a life that somehow seemed stronger the weaker his body got, the closer that storm came. Seeing him like that, the strength in him, it made me love him more.

## GUIDE DOG

For hours I lay there and told him everything, all of these things, so much more. Sometimes he sighed, sometimes he looked in my direction. There are a lot of people that think animals can understand us, or sense our emotions, something – I don't know. I really think he was trying to comfort me. At one point I stopped talking and fell asleep. And in my sleep he was there with me.

We were in a field, a place we had gone for walks fewer times than I would have liked. Billy sat bolt upright and alert, like he'd chase down a squirrel in about three bounds. He looked me right square in the eyes and tilted his head to the side. "I didn't move myself in the way of that car because somebody trained me to."

It hadn't occurred to me yet that I was dreaming, I just about fell over backward because my dog was talking to me. His head straightened and he continued, "I didn't do it because somebody convinced me to be that sort of dog. I didn't do it for the reward of a treat, or a pat on the head." Billy stood up and started walking toward me. "I did it because a world where we focus on ourselves will die before we do." As he came closer he seemed to grow so that he was as tall as me and standing at arm's length. "But a world where we take the opportunity to reach out and help each other, lend an ear, or help a blind woman cross the road, is a world full of hope and love."

The world around me spun, pulling me in every direction at once until it refocused, leaving us in the middle of an intersection. I saw a young, healthy Billy leading a woman down the sidewalk at the corner of 96th. An SUV revved its engine, swerved around the very spot where I was standing, and went straight for that woman. Then Billy was there with a short bark and pushed the woman backward, taking the full impact as the breaks squealed. I stood there unharmed and terrified that the car had actually been trying to avoid *me*. I was frozen to the spot. My friend walked past me up to a ruined dog lying in the road and studied his past self. He turned and looked at the woman who had fallen to the ground, who was getting to her feet with the help of a couple strangers asking if she was alright.

"I did it because – when she came into the training facility and I saw her, I just loved her and wanted to keep her safe." The woman scrambled back to the pavement, feeling around frantically with both hands for her savior, crying out his name. "Life isn't something you sell, my friend." She screamed to him, buried her face into his coat, and sobbed. Billy turned back to me and said, "Life is something you give."

I woke up with a gasp, both hot and cold from sweating. In those few moments where a dream mixes with the real world I saw that my friend lay on his pillows and blankets just as he was when I fell asleep. I saw that he hadn't moved, that he wasn't moving. He wasn't even breathing. There was a sound from near the bedroom door that might have been a bark but sounded more like somebody was saying "Bark!" And Billy was there by the door, pawing at the frame to get out. When I rubbed my eyes clear the worlds separated, one waxed and one waned, the real world closing in with loneliness.

## FROM THE HEART

That was the day I buried my friend.

The next morning played the same tricks on my mind, and Billy scratched at the door to be let out. "Bark!" he yelled at me, and vanished. Again the next morning, and the next. Tears replaced the dryness in my eyes at the start of every day.

On the day a full week had passed, and Billy yelled at me in the morning, I called out to him not to go. "Stay boy!" I yelled, and clung to the dream that he was. He scratched at the door and sat down. He looked at me and panted. He wagged his tail and waited. I got out of my bed and expected him to be gone at every blink. In the end I laughed a little; the poor guy hadn't been out to pee in a week. So I put on some clothes, opened the door, and we went for a walk.

There was no leash. Nobody stepped to the side when we passed. And after a while I was glad there was no mess to clean up. "This is life," he said. Morning sun, a fresh breeze of air, a city full of people still waking. He was right. I said it back to him, "This is life." I wished every day could be the same.

We came up to a corner where a road led to the heart of the city, where the traffic was heavier with daily commutes, where I wasn't paying attention to anything but the life that the morning had brought me. I walked along the last few squares of sidewalk where they met with the blacktop pavement while the clouds had my attention, lazy puffy things dotting a blue sky. I put one foot out into the road without thinking to check what might or might not be coming toward me, stumbling forward when the pavement was an inch lower than I expected, and Billy yelled at me again, "BARK!", and something yanked me backward by my shirt. My heart jumped into my throat, the images he showed me in a dream flew through my mind, and something collided with my side.

A woman gasped in surprise as both of us fell to the ground. "I'm so sorry!" she yelled, before the tumbling had even come to a stop. I scrambled back to my feet and looked around to take in what had happened. The woman had dropped a book and a pair of sunglasses. Billy was gone.

"I wasn't paying attention," I said, "let me help you." I reached out my hand, she reached out her hand. Our hands didn't quite meet in the middle. "I'm Eric," I said and extended my hand a little farther. I helped her stand up, she brushed off her clothes, and I set to picking up the things she dropped.

"No really, it's my fault. I thought I heard – something," she said. I collected her glasses, slightly scratched, and book, which appeared to be untitled. "I daydream a lot when I should be more careful. It's a long story. There's been a lot of things going on in my life the last few years and sometimes I just – overshare with complete strangers. Sorry." She laughed a little. A light trill of a happy thing.

She was very kind for somebody who had just been knocked down. And very pretty, for whatever appearances matter. I offered her the book and sunglasses, she reached out a hand and

## GUIDE DOG

didn't take them. "And my name, it's Clarke. Nice to meet you." I took her hand for the second time, noticing the softness of her skin and feeling the warmth of her smile. She held up a walking stick I hadn't noticed, "This thing just isn't as much help as it could be."

I put her glasses into her hand, she placed them on her face. She took her book, and smiled again. She turned the corner and started to walk away. I didn't want her to walk away, something inside me wanted her to stay. But I didn't know what to say, how to make her want to turn around. "I've got time!" I blurted out.

Clarke turned around, her eyebrows dipping below the frame of her sunglasses, "What? Time for what?"

I closed the space between us with a few quick steps. "I, well, you said that it's a – a long story. You said you were distracted and it's a long story. I'm," I took a breath, offering myself instead of selling myself, "I'm not doing anything right now. I can listen. We can get a coffee."

## FROM THE HEART

I saw her eyebrows raise and I think she held her breath. "You want to get coffee? With me?" Clarke shifted shyly, a timid smile turned to a blush. "Ok. Yes. Yes that would be really nice."

"There's a place about a block away" I said, "I can smell it from here." I hesitated for a moment, my heart beat like I was running. Possibly the boldest thing I've ever done in my life was to reach out and take her hand just then for the third time, of what would be hundreds, possibly thousands. I gently took the walking stick and put my own hand in its place. She closed her fingers around my own and she trusted me. Together we walked back to where we had run into each other. We walked across the road. And then – we kept on walking.

# IMMORTAL

I believe. In fact, I believe in an awful lot of things:

*Past lives and souls, the heartbeat of time,*

*spirits both angry and kind,*

*the sun and the moon and a billion billion stars,*

*and the power of heart and mind.*

It's sort of a mantra of mine. Since the day I first thought it up I've added Immortality. I believe in forever. Not the kind that is indestructible, but the kind that can always stay. Love and happiness can be brought to ruin, or it can go on and on; very much as life from an Immortal *can* be taken, or be left to go on through the ages. I believe in all of these things because of where my life has taken me and what roads I have traveled. So many roads. And of Immortals, I know one. Stoic yet soft, intent yet yielding, harsh yet charismatic. Some of all things, I should imagine; and likely from enduring all things. If life doesn't rub off on you just a bit, you're probably doing it wrong.

I believe, also, that I am what I see in the world. The more good I wish to see in myself, the more I look for it. It makes me happy, and it helps me grow. But the mood of the world I pull from has an ebb and flow, a wax and a wane; and so too, everyone has bad days, even if most are good. I like to think most have been good.

I know an Immortal, and I have for some time. Sixty-five years it has been, of mostly good; though certainly we have had our differences and our indifferences, we have had our in-betweens. And of those good and captured moments that fill the pages of an album, oh how beautiful the wedding was, I find it difficult to look when the only thing that changes - is me. It is perhaps not as obvious if those around you develop in the same ways, hunch in the same bones, and wrinkle in the same lines, but I am old. I am not horribly inconvenienced by these things, except that I do worry about remaining appealing enough. Not in a vain way, no not that. I feel I am being outgrown the more I grow out. Indeed, I will soon be outlived. And someday, replaced.

Oh, I will very soon be outlived.

Photographs. Aren't they a wonderful thing? They can capture so much of a single instant in time, so many good days, good moments. We don't make habit of remembering the bad ones; we learn by those moments and leave them to forgotten history. It is, I believe, the power of the heart and mind. But imagine the photographs you would find in the possession of those Immortal. Think of the time and the ages they have seen. Such that extends so far beyond the recordings of photographs, winding back through sketches in pencil, drawings in charcoal, and oil on canvas. What variety there might be among those faces! Each crest in the ocean of time a wrinkle or grey hair, progressing through the images until, suddenly, replaced with a new one. The tide comes in and the tide goes out, always following the moon, always warmed by the sun, and always reflecting the stars in the darkness.

I feel as though they are always watching, all of those faces, even from the boxes in which they have been stored. I feel they are regarding me for better or for worse, and are pleased or vengeful. They are kind to me for what we have shared, or perhaps angry with me for what I have taken as my own: my unchanging Immortal. Our unchanging Immortal. Those eyes that do not change in any medium, that oil and charcoal and pencil somehow captured as perfectly as a camera, they undo me. Even beside another face, those eyes undo me. And I feel for those that age at the side of the Immortal, I really do. I feel their loss and anguish, I feel their pulling-at-the-seams. Oh reckless time that beats on and onward, leaving us to perhaps be but moments to learn by, to be left to forgotten history. It is a cadence, that onward beating, and it is ceaseless; like an anxious moment of the heart it quickens, and like a sigh it slows.

For all those moments that I am built upon,

# IMMORTAL

for all that I see and have seen in the world, that I am what I have seen, I am now, in the end, old and worn and frail. Such as the world truly is. I notice the cracks in the dirt between the rains, and I notice the darkness of the clouds when it does rain. I notice the pang of hunger between meals, and I notice the nauseating manner in which we chew, like the cud of a cow but with the single added grace of lips to conceal the sight. I have noticed much since I found the papers and pages and portraits. Perhaps what I am in the world is but a simple face after all. For those faces, they do more than age in the same manner from one tide of life to the next, in some way they are very nearly *repeated* faces, as though a memory were trying to be replaced time and again since the age of the first. Since the first with black hair and light skin, with thin lips and a narrow nose, with a kind smile and gentle brow. For all of my mortal life I have tried and strived, struggling through it all, to remain a good soul. But these papers and pages and portraits lend to the belief that I was found as a piece to collect. In some decades my maturing will be seen, aging understood, wrinkling pitied, and dry earth skin sighed about when my Immortal takes another, who will one day find my photographs. And then another. And yet another. And on and on.

Arthritis nearly robbed me of a makeshift noose, and knobby knees almost kept me on the floor, but triumphantly I stand with the soft hem of the bed skirt tied around my neck. I used to think I had something inside, something that caught the attention of a creature that knew how to find it. I stand now to break but a spoke in the wheel of the cycle, which is now laid out across the floor before me. Papers. Pages. Portraits leaned against the wall. And it rings with beautiful poetry that a mirror, mounted to the wall, frames what is left of me. I will very soon be outlived.

So I look at myself, as I feel I have been looked at. I don't like what I see. An image, mounted and framed, of dying and despair. I look into myself, as a younger version of me learned to do by habit. And in the reflection, within my eyes, I can see my soul. It will find better things than to be collected. I take from this world my body, my shell. I wish that the remaining thing of beauty within may somehow be freed. It will be like an excavation of a desert realm, an ancient temple full of wonder will be unearthed from the rain starved land that is my flesh.

That is why I kick. That is why I break the spoke. That is why I swing gently. Back and forth. With the still unsubsiding desire to find good in the world so that I might become it, if for but one final moment, my eyes, where the soul peers out from, look around at the eyes scattered across the floor and against the walls. I find that the same eyes stare back. No, it is the same happiness that stares back. The same *soul* stares back at me. And I remember that I believe, too, in past lives.

And I believe, swinging gently, like a last dance, that my Immortal believes:

*In past lives and souls. The heartbeat of time.*

*Believes in spirits both angry and kind.*

*The sun and the moon and a billion billion stars.*

## FROM THE HEART

*And the power of heart and mind.*

I cannot whisper, "I am sorry," to the empty room full of us.

And I cannot whisper, "I hope you find me again."

# PHONOGRAPH

A gentle waltz serenades the sun to sleep. A hunched old man kisses a wrinkled old woman. Their feet never miss a step, not a beat. She smiles her cheeks and kind eyes into youthfulness. She wears a dress that hasn't seen the light in over a decade. Time completely slips away and leaves them be while the music wisps and slinks around their heels and arms.

"Oh, Albert. I remember this song. The band played this on our first date. My, my. That was so long ago. Wasn't it? Two foolish teenagers without a care in the world." Her voice isn't as strong as it once was; gravely and somewhat strained, yet still sweet as sugar, and smooth as silk. Just one of the things he always loved about her.

Albert smiles. "Yes, a long while now. Took me quite some time to find this song, if I may take credit for the hard work of tracking it down. Most of all, it gives me an excuse to take your hand and have this dance."

"Always, my dear. You may always have a dance."

He rests his head against hers, temple to temple, silently thinking the same words, words that don't need saying. They have always known one another's mind, as they know now. Words like, "I love you", and "Isn't tonight wonderful?", and "I miss you terribly".

Her hair holds memories; he brushes it behind an ear. Her sway brings calm; he allows it to lull him. Her perfume carries nostalgia; he breathes it in deep, until he too is young again.

The song draws to its conclusion, the roll on the player slows to a stop, and the warmth in his arms slips away as his wife fades into the very air she graced. Even the smell of her perfume leaves him, in his living room, quite alone.

Albert sighs low, lowering his arms down to

his sides. He makes his way to the easy chair, dark blue and worn, patting a wooden box with letters from his wife as he sits. His knowledge-steeped eyes, now wandering and wet, cast themselves aimlessly on the vacant corners of his room. Some moments pass, and the old man sighs again. The grandfather clock in the dining room chimes the hour, echoing against sparsely hung walls, and silence resumes.

There were good days, and there were bad days. Mostly there were simply days, and they were with her. Now endless amounts of days just come and go. Nothing in life is a pressing matter anymore, with nothing to look forward to, and nothing to regret.

From somewhere in the distance of the fog that seems to dwell in his mind, a knocking sound emanates, and persists, only pulling his attention away from his thoughts when it refuses to cease. His eyes focus on the front door and he knows he'll have to get up, if only to make it stop.

"Goodness gracious dad! I almost called the

hospital. What are you doing in there?"

"Good evening to you too, sweetheart. Where's my grandkid?" He claps his hands together expectantly.

"Dad. It's a dog. And I didn't have room for him this time. Actually, I'm running late. Do you have that stuff you wanted me to pick up?" She is a near spitting image of her mother. Albert, unintentionally, tends to avoid looking straight at her these days. It is rather an uncomfortable feeling for him, who he sees in his daughter's eyes.

He motions for her to come in, "Yeah, the box is just in here."

She hefts the large box up into her arms and turns to the door. "Why don't you get yourself a nice young fella' to help you with things like that?" He asks, not unkindly.

His daughter laughs. "I'm 62 and can handle myself. ...old man." This makes Albert smile. With a wink, she asks, "What about you? Are you seeing anyone?"

# PHONOGRAPH

"Oh, sometimes." His eyes drift to the phonograph in the corner. "Sometimes."

She catches his sidelong glance and follows his eyes to the old thing. "My goodness! Is that the one Rick found for you? I can't believe what wonderful condition it's in. Oh, could we listen to a song? I'm quite sure I could make time for a song... I-"

"Another time, perhaps," he says, with a shortness that he doesn't intend. "A little tired, I'm afraid." She nods an understanding and walks back across the living room.

Albert gets the door for her, the door squeaks as he opens it full. "You take care of yourself dad." She kisses him on the cheek, looks at him thoughtfully, holding a thought for a moment before dismissing it, and shuffles down the steps with the box of her mom's old things.

The sound of her car engine becomes distant, and once again he is left in quiet. Quiet is one thing he can never get used to. The silence stuffs his ears, the stillness unsettles him, and the loneliness gnaws at him. He can't help but look again to the corner where the phonograph sits on a small table.

Old bones and weak knees carry him over to the cabinet where he keeps his small stock of rolls, smelling like things aged. He sometimes wonders if he has the same sort of smell. Of age. Carefully he picks a song and removes it from the padded cup, switching it with the one he had played earlier. More tenderly than china he holds them, and more precious than gemstones he treats them.

"I do believe," he says to himself, "that this is the song I was thinking of just now." His fingers bulge at the knuckles, and his fingers tremble slightly, and he manages to set the needle. "Our wedding song. How beautiful you looked that night… Another dance, my dear?" As the music begins to play, he turns to the middle of the room and holds out his hand.

A flowing white garment slips into the middle

of the room, a sweet perfume fills the air, and a hand gently sets into his. "One more, Albert. You may always have one more dance."

# KING NAJRA

There was a man called Najra, who was King of a great land that stretched for many hundreds of miles. A river wound from one end to the other, bringing water to his people. As with all rivers, in some places the water rushed and eddied, in others it trickled and pooled. His wondrous palace sat on flat land, and so the river was peaceful there.

All in his garden was good to be eaten; from the many beautiful flowers to the small fruits on the ordinary trees. Herbs and vegetables grew upon and in the earth. Many servants tended the garden that made the king happy, and he was thankful to the river for all that it brought him. But his palace was an Oasis and was surrounded by dry lands and small dusty villages.

"Such beauty ought not to be drowned out!" He thought.

## KING NAJRA

Rare and colorful were the exotic varieties of blooming flowers that shone in the warmth of day. The trees that surrounded the garden and drew close to the river were of a lush green, but of quite a common type.

"Such beauty is not to be drowned out!" He whispered.

Now it came to pass one year that the air was particularly dry, and crops particularly sparse. King Najra invited the important families of the land to dine with him in his garden beside the cool river. A young woman of remarkable wonder in the King's eyes was walking along paths, cooled and fed by his servants.

"Such beauty will not be drowned out!" He proclaimed.

He at once set out to make her Queen and vowed to know nothing but beautiful things.

The servants were made to wear brilliant blues, reds, and yellows. "See how you may compare to the garden, and my Queen." And they soiled the clothes upon the earth in their toils, for prosperous things indeed require great labors.

The trees he called to be pulled from their roots saying, "See how they are plain in my garden, and drink the water from my river, robbing these flowers." And the hot sun beat down where shade had been and dried up the river where it was calm, and it no longer flowed. The garden and his precious oasis crumbled to dust also, for wondrous things indeed require the greatness of other things.

Now, Najra desperately wanted to look upon his Queen's face, and behold the only beauty that was left to him, but he could not. She was gone from him and left only a note on a small piece of parchment saying, "Beauty is neither a thing to behold in contrast to lesser things, nor to behold in the presence of greatness alone; for there is beauty in all things. It is because you fail to know this that you too will surely crumble to dust amidst your sand dunes and withered river bed."

## KING NAJRA

The King did not heed the warnings brought before him, and he set out in search for his queen throughout all that was left to him. Among his sand dunes and withered river bed, he searched until, lost with no direction and parched as the desert, he could go no further. The King bent, collapsed, and became dust atop a high dune. As the winds carried him away, the sun sank to the horizon and spread an array of colors beyond imagine, across the entire sky. It was drowned out by an ordinary black sky ...marked with millions of gleaming stars.

Thus Najra was remembered as the King who would not see not see beauty.

# THE TREE IN CONCORD PARK

I couldn't tell you what the point of life is, and anybody that says they know is only telling you how they justify the life they're already living. Or wish they were living. That said, the best I can do is tell you how I wish I was living my life; because, as it stands, I'm not living much of one at the moment. We all need a goal, something to aspire to, something to wake up for in the morning. For now, the point of my life is a tree just off the path that winds through Concord Park.

It's true that a tree doesn't need very much help. Actually, the point of a tree is that it doesn't need help. You see, they've got everything they need right there, reaching up, digging down, growing itself for the purpose of being bigger.

Roots; they pull food and water out of the

# THE TREE IN CONCORD PARK

ground. Leaves; they make food from the sun and give it to the tree. The roots grow bigger so the tree can grow bigger so it can hold more leaves. You see? It doesn't need me at all to do what it does. We're connected, nonetheless. This old tree and me. Not just because I put it there 50 years ago.

50 years ago it was just a bit taller than me. Of course I was 15 at the time, and Concord Park was just being made. The land was full of garbage and heavy brush; my old man bought the land and set out to make it a place for families to go. It was the point of his life. His reason for waking up in the morning - family. Not just his, everybody's. The whole community pitched in, and everybody had a point in life for a few years. They made it beautiful. And they named it Concord Park. Concord, you're probably thinking, is a grape; those nice fat purple ones that make second rate wine and which everybody puts in their pies. The word means "*Peace*".

Dad let me pick the last tree, and he let me pick where it would go. On the path, one and a half miles of it, there was a small bare spot where a picnic table might have gone. I was already connected to it, that patch of earth, and it wanted me to be there. I decided to dig the hole myself, couldn't even tell you how long it took me to do it, and a couple of men came with the tree on the back of a truck. After they dropped it in I cut the twine around the burlap that protected the roots and the soil that clung to it, heavy and black, rich and smelling of an old forest.

They told me I might just have dug the hole too far off the path, but I knew deep down that someday that tree would grow bigger than any other in the park and would need that extra space. I think I just wanted the tree to have what I wanted – space. Room to breathe. Room to stretch out my roots. Those two men drove off long before I set out. I just sat there with the tree. It breathed in my carbon dioxide, and I breathed in its oxygen; something I remembered from school, I figured it made us symbiotic somehow. I also remembered about some little shrimp thing in the ocean that puts off more oxygen than trees, and that if all the trees in the world died we would still have enough fresh air. So no, we didn't do much for each other. But a life force was there, and it wound around the both of us.

Six years later the tree had shot right up, the leaves had spread out, and I – I stopped sitting under it. An education, you see, had to be obtained several states away. Whenever I got homesick over the following years – that tree was why.

Four more slipped by, years that is, and I accrued more debt than knowledge. I gave up, basically. What was the point in learning all that stuff, anyway? Someday, I knew, I'd die and my head full of things would be worth as much as a muddy boot.

I went home. Home to my sick dad. Home to Concord Park. Home to my tree. And wouldn't you know it, I found the point of my life for the next thirty years sitting under that tree, eating a sandwich, a book perched on her knees. Oh, we talked for hours untold; until, eventually, the sun came back up, and I walked her home. In the end, she wanted to get married under that tree. I told her we could surely decide on a better place with a little more room for others to gather around. In the end she won out, and the ceremony was small. That day was the last time my dad was able to leave the house. For that, I never second guessed my wife again.

I handled it alright, my dad passing away. It took strength but I was able to work through it, to just sigh and breathe through it. That worked alright for me until the day we learned we couldn't have kids. I needed him that day, I really did. I even caught myself dialing his number.

After trying for so long to have a baby I finally said we could go to the doctor to find out if it was possible, but that the doctor was never allowed to tell us who it was that couldn't have kids. The only thing worse than finding out I couldn't give her a child would be to watch her heartache if she couldn't bear. I nodded my head, with a lump in my throat, when she told me she wanted to bury a small token under the tree where

# THE TREE IN CONCORD PARK

the child that could never be, would never be. Five and a half weeks later my wife got sick one morning. She "just knew", and she tested positive for pregnancy. Now I've cried out of sadness before, but that might have been the first time I ever did cry out of joy.

The thing about Concord Park in the summer is that it's the greenest place I've ever seen. Even after traveling across four states for college. The green is ever-changing, from bright to deep. And, oh, when the leaves change color in the fall, well the world has never seen so many colors. Some even go to a deep purple. They crinkle under foot along the paths and the light plays through the newly open places in the branches. Even if you've been hiking to a thousand places, I think I can safely say you've never seen a place like Concord (Peace) Park.

The leaves were falling like Autumnal snow that first time we brought our daughter, whose nickname is Shade, to the tree. The trees would soon rely on their roots for what little food they could get during the winter months, having shed all of their leaves. Why nature would design something to just fall apart like that I don't think I could ever imagine. But then again, I know I've done the same thing. My leaves just fell away when I went away to college, when I lost my dad, and when our child could never be; the sadness crunching under my defeated steps. And I've also grown a full new set of leaves time and again. But right then, in that place and with my family, I had never felt so completely and utterly alive in all my life.

I don't know where I would be right now if it hadn't been for our child, the sweet impossible child that was; but if it was still someplace on this earth, it would be a place without leaves. As I said, that woman sitting on the grass with a sandwich and a book was my point in life for 30 years. And when those years were over I was lost beyond measure. I had very little keeping my feet on the ground. Our girl, she was my roots. I fear I made myself be the point of her life for too long, taking care of me and getting me up every morning. She gave me something to do,

## THE TREE IN CONCORD PARK

something to add purpose, and it was to care for the tree.

That tree gave me the life I have. And so I would do the same for the rest of my years. I would always stay there a while where my wife lay beneath the branches, nestled in the roots, to tell her I love her still.

When at last my beautiful "Shade" decided it was time to leave home she asked me to go on a walk through the park with her. It was in the fall, and the leaves fell like rain on her hair, and the light again played through the newly open places in the branches. I cut a small piece from the tree and told her to find a place to grow it. I told her it would be her roots, and it would be her leaves. She said, "No, dad. You are."

50 years ago it was just a bit taller than me, when Concord Park was just being made, and dad let me pick that last tree. I picked a Weeping Willow. The leaves had made me think of my mother's hair, you see. And our daughter's name is Willow. And whenever I feel like the wind is

## FROM THE HEART

blowing too hard on my life, like I'm losing my leaves again, my Weeping Willow cries for me. I go to the park, and walk along a well-worn path to the place, so long ago, I chose. I walk through the curtain of trailing branches into a cool and separate world. I reach my hand out to its side, and the wind blows, and the leaves shudder…

# FIREBOX

I cough and gag, I wheeze; a sharpness fills my nose, throat, and lungs, and I can't think straight. I draw in short gasps of awful air that continues to add to the nails clawing at my windpipe. And the heat - the unbearable heat. Red-orange flames gorging on furniture all around me, flailing their arms and arguing over the best way to cook my flesh. My mind won't clear, and the diminishing oxygen weakens my limbs which lay helplessly around me on the hot floor. I'm going to die right here, in some living room with black-burned walls.

My heartbeat pounds against my chest, wasting what little life my being has left. Thump. Thump. Thump. Such regularity and rhythm my pulse has left. Thump. Thump. Smash!

"Over here! I need help over here! I found somebody!"

## FROM THE HEART

Enormous padded hands grab hold of me, and a muffled voice says, "Come on!" and, "I'll get you out of here!" His face is hidden behind a reflection of the horror surrounding us, and I squint my eyes closed against the brilliant colors and smoke.

Past tattered remnants of a wall, through an entryway, and out a door we stumble, before my legs collapse beneath me. The gloves catch my weight, pulling me across the street. New hands in latex gloves, gentle and precise, place a mask over my mouth and my lungs take in the new air, pure and fresh. Tears are streaming down my face, no doubt cleaning thin rivulets as they wash away the soot. I look to the house with the black plumage, illuminated by flashing reds and blues. I search up and down the street trying to grasp where I am and what has happened, the shock of it all shuddering through my body.

I'm hit by an even worse realization than that promise of death I was pulled from; I am waking to an unknown existence. I feel like this is the point where my life should flash, scene to scene, before my eyes. But no memories come.

All I can remember is a small box, black, matte. A slightly dulled silver keyhole. An entire life represented by a single object. But I know, by some grace, that it is *my* life that lies within that box.

"Is there anybody else in the house?" The voice is demanding. It hitches and breaks. "Are you alone?" My own face, so charred and battered, is now reflected the mask, creating the illusion that I am my own savior. The blank expression I see looking back at me might tell him the truth; that I don't know if anybody is still in the house. All I know for certain is that I've lost myself, the one thing that can't be pulled from the increasing rubble before us. He turns to the house.

The hands in latex gloves help me to sit on something cushioned. Then questions. Questions about me and does anything hurt. Everything is numb. I close my eyes against the fog of confusion. The box, black, matte, with a slightly dulled silver keyhole, appears once again in my mind. It calls to me. It beckons me. My memory is frail as a tattered cloth, but this box is tangible. It has definite dimensions to it, and it has a weight. I know that I have the key; that slightly dulled silver. I reach out, and touch it.

\*  \*  \*

*"Are you kidding me? Do you really think we need one of these?" I ask.*

*She looks at me with serious and burning eyes and I know she's not kidding at all. She's right, really. It's just that money is so tight. But if I say that she'll flip for certain. Her eyes soften and she asks, "What if something was to happen to one of us, or both of us? I need to know that the important things are kept safe. Like our wills."*

*"We haven't got wills yet." Someday I'll learn when not to correct her. Unfortunately, it isn't today.*

*"Well we would have, if YOU had contacted the lawyer a MONTH ago like you SAID you were going to." She doesn't yell, as much, we're in the store after all. But there is definitely scorn in her voice. I beat myself up*

*inside again for being so damn forgetful all the time.*

"Yes, you're right. I – I'm sorry hon." I sigh. *And she is right, even if it feels like nagging.* "I know we need something like this." *She spins her head back to me and glares. I had apologized for the lawyer thing, and she had let it go; then I had to go and say "something LIKE this".*

*She turns back to the shelf and looks between the two models and asks, flatly,* "Padlock, or key?" *I know full well I'd forget the stupid number. I know full well I'd forget where we put the key. Either way, if something happens to her, whatever goes into this thing is a lost cause. Unless we can use our anniversary date, or imbed the key into my skin... No. Basically the world needed her to survive to open this thing no matter what. My hesitation draws a sigh and she answers herself,* "Key it is then."

*She reaches up and begins to pull the firebox from the shelf, above her head.*

"Sweetheart!" *I all too sternly intervene.* "You know *you shouldn't be lifting heavy things."*

*"I hope you're being chivalrous and not patronizing."*

## FROM THE HEART

*I grab the firebox from the shelf and hide a huff of surprise at its weight. I turn my body, the box leaning away from her, and kiss her. She understands my intention and smiles warmly, massaging her protruding belly.*

\*         \*         \*

"Sir, please. Is there anybody else in there?!" My eyes snap open.

"I - I don't know. I think maybe." My words sound distorted through the oxygen mask. "I'm sorry." My shoulders slump in defeat.

Determined, and selflessly fulfilling his duty, he takes off toward the house in a full out sprint. I squeeze my eyes shut, hoping for an answer to his question.

As though looking through the eyes of a fly, I can see the box from every angle at the same time. How many times must I have held it in my hands? Turned it over? Opened it? The feel of the key in my hand finds me. The way the small tool is chilled at the touch, and quickly warms as I hold it. Teeth up, a little wiggle to fit it in right, and I unlock it with a grinding clockwise twist. On weary hinges I lift the lid. Its contents explode and wisps of a life scatter all around me.

Some things I know belong and some things do not. Rather they did belong at one time and have been taken out to make room for a new something. I reach out and grab an item; a small, dark blue leather booklet with perhaps a dozen or so pages. Gold colored inlay covers the front with words.

\*         \*         \*

*"I hereby commence the first sorting-of-the-box ceremony; may there be many more to come." Our glasses chink a little louder than we mean. There has already been a bit of red wine during the pre-ceremony, and she giggles a little at the whole thing. I have to admit, the candle is a nice touch, and it makes her hair absolutely radiant; and the glinting of the dancing flame in her eyes…*

*The wine glass is in her right hand. She picks the key up with her left hand and fumbles at the lock. I shake my head a little and turn my finger in clockwise circles.*

## FROM THE HEART

*My wife winks ridiculously at me and sets down her things, picking them up in turn with the opposite hands. Then she fumbles at the lock with her right hand.*

*I reach forward and lift the lid, which I had already unlocked when she refilled our glasses. Probably, if she was any closer, she'd slap me. Instead she sips her wine again and reaches into the box to see what can be removed, permanently.*

*Our recently used social security cards are set on her side of the box; I've just landed myself a new job and we needed the cards to apply for the new insurance that came with it. I can only assume this is going to be the "keep it" pile.*

*Out come our passports with the fake leather texture that is actually blue plastic, the word 'Passport' embossed in gold lettering, a dozen or so pages to hold the stamps of all the places in the world you've been... but we don't open them. There aren't any stamps in them, and they expired three months ago. These things are good for ten years. Ten years have gone by and we missed out on our one-year-of-dating cruise (for a scheduling conflict), our honeymoon to Mexico (because we both got sick before the trip), and even the recent plans to Canada (which we could have done without a passport only a couple of years ago).*

*She glows, but she doesn't radiate like she usually does. We both feel the sense of loss staring at the booklets. I quietly slide the passports to my side of the table. The flame trembles once or twice, trying to get her attention, but she only swallows at the dryness in her mouth.*

*I pull our birth certificates out next, along with Audrey's. I stop her for a moment to look at the third paper. It feels precious to me, as if it is an actual piece of our daughter. A sip of wine passes my lips and I re-read the numbers and words.*

*Audrey Elizabeth, 6 lbs. 7 oz. 18 ¾ inches. Born on August 4*$^{th}$*, 6:17 pm. 3 years, 6 months, 1 week, 3 days... unless it's late enough now to be Thursday, then it's 4 days...*

*"Six seventeen? I thought it was six twenty-one?"*

*"No, that's when the nurses finally picked you up off of the floor, dear." She snickers into her Merlot as she takes a gulp.*

## FROM THE HEART

*I roll my eyes at her, "Cute. You're really cute, you know that? I'm serious, how did I get that wrong?"*

*She tells me memory isn't my "forte" and drains her glass. I tell her she needs to be done with the wine.*

\*       \*       \*

My wife. My daughter. My Audrey! Panic surrounds and consumes me just as the smoke had moments before. I blink my eyes open and see the fireman only a few paces away in his sprint toward the flames. My memories were mere flashes of thought and feeling; coming together like a jigsaw puzzle, struggling with missing pieces. Hoping for more, searching for more, I squint my eyes tight again and rummage through the box in my mind.

A thick manila envelope, held closed by a red stringed figure-8; we did finally get around to that will after all. A couple of birth announcements, a couple of death announcements. An ownership certificate with a tag.

It's a bone tag, engraved and personalized.

Scruffy Jones, 223 Lennon St. The tag is a similar cool to that of the key, but much smoother.

\*        \*        \*

*He sits up straight and licks her nose three times drawing a cute little giggle.* "Aww, Dad! Look, the puppy looooves me!" *He lays down on the floor and stares up with big innocent eyes, and Audrey crouches down to his level to snuggle against him.*

"This fella is probably a good choice for your little one. He used to belong to an older woman; he's very docile and attentive." *The shop worker crouches down to scratch behind his ear,* "She passed away about two weeks ago, and the family wanted him to go somewhere he could take it easy from now on. They call him Scruffy."

*Scruffy's ears perk up slightly, his big eyebrows shift as he looks in the shop worker's direction. Good dog, smart dog. My wife and I exchange glances. Audrey is already smitten, and Scruffy couldn't be happier than to have the love of this little girl. We know without words that he is the perfect dog. He still has his old collar on. That will have to be changed today so he doesn't get sent to a vacant home if anything should happen. Lennon Street, it says. The woman lived just two streets away from us.*

*I feel a little sad, that I never noticed this woman walking with her dog. There's a lot that I don't notice in life. So much of it just slips right past; the harder I try to hold on, the faster it slides through my fingers. Silently, I decide to keep the old tag in her memory. If Scruffy is going to be a part of our family, that makes her our extended family. Scruffy can keep the collar too, I think he'd like that.*

*"He'll make a great addition to your family. I'll get the papers."*

*Scruffy stands up at attention when Audrey grabs his collar in proud ownership. They walk around the little shop, him in the lead, and she tells him about all the animals they pass. "Look, there's a cute kitty. Do you like kitties, Scruffy? I bet you do. OH! And look at him. He's so cute too! It says he's a sugar gli… glider. Awww." This decision was clearly way above us. This was meant to be. "Do you want to watch the hamsters running, Scruffy? They get pretty good exercise, huh?"*

*Another little girl, not yet 2 years I should think,*

*runs up to Scruffy with ear-to-ear grins and hugs his face. I don't need to worry about how he'll treat her. I'll never have to worry about having a dog that gets mean or too rough. Audrey is just as sweet to the little one, introducing them to each other and asking if they want to be friends too. Three licks on the little one's nose says yes. The little girl giggles and hugs his face again...*

\*     \*     \*

Tickets from our first movie, a couple of CD's full of baby pictures, a set of keys. These are not my keys though; not for my house, not for my car. Whose keys are they? In my mind they have the same coolness to my hands as the box key and the dog tag. How hot must these items be at this moment? Will the papers burn in the box from the heat alone? Will the CD's melt in there? How safe are these memories, and why didn't I care more when we were buying the thing?!

\*     \*     \*

*'Just in case you ever need to stop over and I'm not at home, or if it's late and the door is locked, or whatever the*

*reason. Plus, I think you still have a box of your things in the attic after all these years." My mother will keep going on about the keys if I don't accept them and tell her I'll be sure to use them if I need to.*

*I take the keys from her gesturing hands and look at them, as if looking at them will tell me what door each goes to; front or back, maybe a side door. Concluding that I'll just have to try them all when the occasion arises, I look back at her and smile.*

*"You don't even need to call ahead, honey. And not just for this weekend either. Any time at all you want to come and see your father and I…"*

*"I will ma, I promise."*

*She smiles a large photogenic smile, warm and full of life. Any child of mine is well cared for in her presence. My wife is leaving for the night too; first business trip in her new position. This is the closest thing to a night to myself I've had in… it doesn't matter.*

*Audrey stands on her tippy toes to give me a kiss; it makes her feel bigger, even if I still have to stoop. She takes her pillow and climbs into her car seat in the back, which is forward facing now making any ride all the more fun for her. Scruffy sits on the pavement next to me, at attention as always. I think if I asked him to go to the store for a gallon of milk, he'd do it without question.*

*My sweetheart kisses Audrey and buckles her in. She says a thank you and a goodbye to my mom, closes the door, and waves. She kisses me and climbs into our car, engine running in anticipation. The air is chilled and the smoky exhaust is dense. Evening has begun to set in heavily, but they'll all be gone for a full two days.*

*I watch them both drive down the road, turning opposite directions at the intersection. Scruffy and I look at each other and head back up the driveway. Audrey left the light on upstairs. I'll turn it off when I check on things up there. Scruffy goes to his doghouse and sits down, waiting for me to chain his collar. When the chilly air brings goose bumps to my arms, I call him to come inside with me to stay warm. We walk around the back of the house so I can lock it on our way in. Scruffy hops through the large flap before I get up the steps. Hopefully, it'll be a quiet night.*

\*          \*          \*

They're out. They went away! I know by some grace that it was last night. They're gone and they're safe! My eyes fly open and the man is almost across the street. I pull the oxygen mask from my face and yell, "Wait! Don't! They're not in there!"

The man who is about to risk his own life stops suddenly in his tracks and turns to me, tension in his muscles like an animal ready to turn and bolt in either direction. I look reassuringly at him to call it off, to save him from risking everything for nothing. The man lifts his visor and I see a real face for the first time. He's just a kid, for crying out loud. Not yet in his mid-twenties!

I wave him back to me with urgency. A moment's hesitation before he scampers back to my side. "The family dog – he must have gotten out the back." I think he's a dog owner because I can suddenly see the sadness in his eyes. Pets are family. I just can't bring myself to think that our dog has as much value to the world as this young man.

# FIREBOX

I think he would have done it, if I asked him to. I think he would have done it if I hadn't stopped him. I hope his parents are properly proud of him.

I wonder now what I smell, what furniture and photos have disintegrated to cause the odor that penetrates the air without the oxygen mask over my nose. How a small box can be expected to hold enough memories in the case of a fire is beyond me. Granted, we will still be able to access the little money in our savings without the melted cards on the kitchen table. The clothes on my body will keep me warm until the morning. And my Audrey has a pillow with her to sleep on in the weeks to follow. But our whole house could be a giant firebox and it still wouldn't contain everything we are and believe.

The time it takes to consume a house depends on what is in it. It makes me wonder how long our home will take, and just how long it has already been ablaze. Shadows set against the flames; my lawnmower is off to the side near the driveway, a small bicycle leans against training wheels in the middle of the lawn, surrounded by tall grass where I refused to mow around it.

\*  \*  \*

*"Come on, kiddo. You can do this. I promise I'll hold on. I won't let go unless you say you're ready to try it by yourself." We tell our children not to ever lie, no matter what. Then we go and lie to them on the pretense that it's for their own good and that they'll learn to trust themselves. But what if the lesson she takes instead is that daddy lied and that's why her knee is bleeding?*

*Audrey looks at me, and considers the possibility that it might happen that way. My girl trusts me to hold on - to do what is best for her. Daddy, she thinks, has never failed her before and he won't start now. I swallow my guilt and smile at her. She puts her feet on the pedals and I coax her forward.*

*My wife calls to us from the partially opened screen door to be careful. She pokes her head out, but her legs stay in, keeping Scruffy (a mere shadow through the door at this angle) inside. I nod my head in her direction. I know to be careful – trust me I'm being careful.*

## FIREBOX

*"Good, good. Just keep your eyes forward and keep pedaling. Relax your arms like we said." She moves her feet down to the ground, up again, down to the ground, until she's doing it. "Just keep pedaling sweetie, you've got this." Around her feet go, and around, and she teeters and begins her fall.*

*But I'm still holding her seat, she doesn't tip far and she doesn't fall down. Her hands are a little white from holding onto the handles so tightly, but her daddy has her safe and secure. Audrey's shoulders droop when she stops pedaling. She wanted so badly to make it. A small face turns to me and she says that sometimes daddy's have to let their kids do things on their own. That she loves me so much but she thinks she can do it. "Let go when I say," she says, determinedly.*

*Her little shoes rest again on the pedals and she starts to move along the sidewalk. The handlebars wiggle this way and that way and straighten with a jerk. "Let go daddy! Let go!" My muscles fight me and don't want to, I don't want to let my baby go and grow up, to ride away from me, to not need daddy. The seat wrenches clear of my hand and off she sails, one sidewalk tile away, two sidewalk tiles. "Let GO daddy! I can do it. I can!" Ten feet away, eleven, twelve, and she falls to the left. Her helmet bounces on the grass and her elbow is scraped, the bicycle pins her leg and she panics just a little.*

*She wriggles out from the bike and looks back at me. Her eyes bulge wide and her jaw falls, "I DID it daddy! I DID it!!"*

\*　　　　　　　　\*　　　　　　　　\*

I'm so glad now that she rode away last night, in grandma's car. Not to grow up, but so grandma could keep her young. Not to go away from me, but to safety. Our lives aren't really in the small box, and they're not really in the house. Our lives are in each other, growing. Her training wheels might be off but she still looks to me for learning. And she knows when to trust me to hold on and when to tell me to let go. Her training wheels - are off.

Oh God. I gawk at the small tipping bike in the yard. What? Then...

\*　　　　　　　　\*　　　　　　　　\*

*The candle on the table flickers again. She stares at*

*the passports one more time and wishes some things had been different. The empty glass turns in her fingers for a moment. She stands up from the chair, bumping her belly against the edge. I catch something of a whisper, an apology to the baby, and she walks into the kitchen.*

\*         \*         \*

*The little girl with blond hair in the pet shop looks at Audrey and lets Scruffy lick her face, and she giggles with delight. She says, "Puppy licking me!" She looks straight at me smiles with little rounded teeth. "Puppy licking me." What a cute kid. "Lick daddy!" she yells, pointing Scruffy in my direction and our new dog trots over to meet me.*

\*         \*         \*

*As they drive away, I look up to the window where Audrey's light was left on. We're always telling that child to turn off the lights, flush the toilet, and wash her hands. I don't like being outside while my little one is sleeping, it feels like anything could go wrong at any time. Audrey and my wife are gone for the night; another calm night, just the two of us and Scruffy.*

\*         \*         \*

## FROM THE HEART

*My wife calls to me from the screen door to "be careful" as if I'm going to mess up something like teaching my daughter to ride a bike. From this angle I can't see more than shadows but I know she's keeping Scruffy back with one leg, and little Samantha with the other.*

\*             \*             \*

There are no training wheels on Audrey's bicycle. It's Samantha's bicycle. My girl. My little girl who is upstairs in there, in that inferno of hellish fire engulfing my house. It waves its crooked fingers towards the heavens so that everyone would know it was victorious over my domain, our place of safety, incinerating to the point of collapse. My heart stops pumping, and my lungs stop breathing, just staring at the shadow of her bicycle in front of the wicked fire.

Something within the house shifts – the sound of a wall collapsing. My feet drop to the ground from my high seat on the stretcher and they take off running, carrying me with them. I'm moving faster than ever before, madly dashing to the front porch to barge back in and get her. My face is the first to take the brunt of the heat which instantly feels like a sunburn and I lunge up the porch steps toward the front door, bracing for the impact and splintering of torched wood.

The young fireman, I think, grabs me by the waist and tears me down to the ground not a pace from the door and wrestles me back, back, back to the street. "SAMANTHAAAA!" Somebody else has my voice, somebody angry and terrified has my voice, somebody desperate and never to be forgiven has my voice and is trying to bring back something that cannot be. "SAAAAMAANTHAAAA!"

He pulls me down hard onto the pavement and something terrified has hold of his body as well. "No, you – you can't." he yells. "It's just… too late. I'm so sorry."

Tears had only just subsided from the sting of the smoke, and now they begin to clean more of the soot from my face. Washing it away. A splintering something shifts loudly inside and I scream, "NOOOOO!" and it's me that has my voice again. Jim. I'm Jim. My wife's name is Sarah. And we have two children. TWO! Another something explodes and the firebox in my mind does the same, all the other memories of who I am swell in a torrent of emotion and swirl around me flashing out of sequence like a soundtrack on shuffle. Sarah. Audrey. Samantha. The fireman pulls me to my feet and back across the street.

"Over there, what is that?" Somebody says.

"Do you see it? Something's moving behind the house!"

"Get over there, now!"

Two people rush back to the fence between the house and the driveway, a shadow or something moving low to the ground. Blankets are thrown, respirators are drawn, a great commotion and rushing back to safety. Our noble Scruffy managed to find his way to the back door where the flap occupied the lower half so that he could come and go. I knew he would find his way out. And still clutching onto the tremendous angel's collar, our faithful servant of a dog, is Samantha. Despite any coaching the firemen do, he brings my daughter straight over to me.

"Daddy! She yells and all that is left of me falls apart, my knees buckle and bash into the ground, every fiber of me shudders. She smiles and throws herself onto me. Her hair is singed all over, and clothes are tattered in several places. "I just knew he would find the way, I knew he would bring me to you, daddy."

The paramedics are all around us, trying to dig in and break apart our embrace to so they can treat her burns and get her oxygen. I loosen my grip so they can tend to her, but she squeezes double hard.

"Don't let go, daddy. Not yet."

# THE WORDS OF ANOTHER

My favorite chair, probably in the whole world, sits where the shade of a tree falls through large bay windows and the smell of fresh brewed coffee wafts by, at Morning Joe. This place is full of regulars and full of new faces. You'd only know the difference by sitting around watching them; the regulars always stick to the same plain coffees, while those that find the place with their smart phone internet searches always go for something more obscure. Also, the regulars walk in shouting "Mornin' Joe!" like Joe is a person and that's where the name comes from.

If you can name it, they have it. I could never pick a favorite, not for anything. Not for "all the tea in China," as they say. But that wouldn't do much for me, I don't drink tea. Never cared much for it. I suppose I could sell all that tea and use the money to buy new kinds of coffee from faraway places; only I imagine that I'd find more flavors to compete with my favorites and I would never be able to decide what to drink. Coffee's not the point I'm trying to make here, though.

They go for the coffee. I go for tranquility. Regardless of our reasons, it seems we all end up in the same place from time to time. And yet I feel like I'm in a world apart, like something is there and they don't notice it. I always wanted to somehow make people see what I see. I always needed to know if it was even possible. That's the sort of point I'm trying to make.

So I go to Morning Joe and hope that my words will flow. Really, the only thing that flows there is the line of customers and the pots of coffee.

It was a day just like all of that. Orders for plain coffee, orders for fancy coffee, new faces, old faces, "Mornin' Joe!". The smells drifting past me and the shade from the tree coming in the bay window on my favorite chair, and I'm ready to write what I see and show every one of these people what they miss every day. Only, no words come to me.

I scribbled a "modern" haiku on the paper:

*Drinking good coffee*

*With pen in hand awaiting*

*And nothing to say*

Not half bad. It didn't seem to get me anywhere either.

I let my mind wander, a waking dream. In this dream I'm outside with a map and shovel, trudging through dense woods. The ink is barely visible on the parchment. But I find this spot, a small clearing, and I plunge the tip of the shovel into the packed earth. I dig earnestly, I dig despairingly, I dig until the sweat drips onto the dusty shovel, which strikes something hard. The shovel falls to the ground, my knees fall to the ground, and I dig with my fingers and nails. An outline reveals itself, rough edges and square. Slowly I pull it free, turning it over to see my treasure, the word my quest is for is engraved on the underside, the word that will help others see.

"Mornin' Joe!"

The dream - the word - burst into a thousand pieces, dispersing among the world it is meant to represent. The sense of loss was immediate to see it scatter; an empty feeling I can only describe as being alone, though of course, no emotion is as simple as a word. Like ash, the remnants settled on the tables, fell into the cups, and caught on the updrafts of steam from hot coffee. They fell on the chairs, onto the customers, and swirled on the tiny breaths of many conversations. And they rested on the hands, and the hair of a new face. They fluttered about in the tiny movements of those eyelashes. Eyelashes that were blinking at me.

There was another sense as immediate as the first. It wasn't a love-at-first-sight thing. I mean, in a way, but that's not the point I'm trying to make. I know what it's like to feel the world and I know what my reflection looks like for it. We saw the same thing in the world. Perhaps even in each other. It felt like meeting a fellow wanderer, a kindred spirit. Of course I quickly looked away.

Back to the paper in front of me. I tried to make more words come, but they were reluctant. To pose as nonchalant, which may have stood out even more, I busied myself with drinking coffee, writing anything at all.

*To the eyes, green, or maybe blue*

*Calm after a storm*

My own eyes are dark. I was writing about somebody else. Somebody else in the coffee house, who was possibly looking at me again - or still. With another sip of coffee, I peered over the rim and through the steam, I saw those eyes again, accompanied by a faint smile. But they are mine for only a moment before being pulled down to pen and paper, coffee and thoughts. Unlike with my own feeble efforts, I watched a pen in the

## THE WORDS OF ANOTHER

hands of another scramble to keep up with the mind that drove it, filling the page as quickly as reading it.

It occurred to me to direct my words to a somebody, to another. To write this thing, a poem, as a gift to one that might appreciate it. To pass it like a secret note, folded ever so carefully, with the words "read me" and a shape less forward than a heart. Perhaps with a smile.

I set down my coffee, picked up the pen, and commanded it to do my bidding.

> *To the eyes, green, or maybe blue*
>
> *The sea after a storm*
>
> *A thought, or maybe feeling*
>
> *To share, conspire, -*

Nothing came to me to rhyme with "storm". I hated that nothing rhymed with storm. And I hated that I wanted to rhyme at all. Always getting caught up in the small details, the things that don't truly matter. My mind barraged me with self-deprecating thoughts and notions; namely that I wasn't good enough. A brief yet detailed history of issues and misses throughout my life came to the surface of my thoughts. No, all negativity aside I wasn't good enough at all. It wasn't a cruel thought, it was simply true. Once I settled on the point, I sighed and stared out the window at the tree.

The breeze, not strong enough to be called wind, fidgeted with the leaves, dropping a few to the ground in a swaying motion; like rocking an infant to sleep, slowly lowering the babe into a cradle. I wanted to feel that way. I wanted it so much that it left me with a pit, or a swelling, in my heart. I wanted everyone to spend the day fascinated by a newly perceived world, and be lulled at night like a baby, gazing at the heavens where there is nothing but infinite wonder.

I turned my attention back to the room, back to the table with the eyes; green, or maybe blue. Only the chair at the table was empty. The same sense of a dream exploding hit me with a jolt, another immediate sense of loss, worse than alone. I always seemed to be getting caught up and missing things, things that matter. Yet there was a detail, a small one, that I picked up on. The table was empty, but not barren. Still sitting there was the saucer, mug, and pad of paper! Perhaps it was nothing more than a restroom break; hope replaced the emptiness.

My entire being was tense, poised, and ready to rush in and rescue the writing pad in the event it was indeed forgotten. But how could such a thing be forgotten? It was impossible. For one last anxious moment I debated. If it was left behind, a barista might come and collect it for their own. Or worse, end all the life in those words by dropping it in a waste bin. Though, if I went for it, I might be caught in what appeared to be theft; less than petty in the eyes of the law, a major offense to the owner. In my thoughts, we both reach for the notebook at the same moment, hands perhaps touching, and I would be left trying to explain myself. It was a terrifying prospect. Yet worse was the thought of not doing so.

## FROM THE HEART

I picked myself up and walked a deliberate stride, staring all the while at the artifact lest it too had been imagined and scatter like another dream. It bore no name, as a personal item might. Merely the words, "For you."

The sound of a car door outside caught my attention; ordinarily it would not, but in such a state of alert, it was impossible to miss. I looked out the front door with only time to catch a sideways glance, a half smile, and one detail on a license plate as it drove out of view. The plate came from out of state, and halfway across the country. How is it that I felt compelled to trek the world in search, when moments before I couldn't even cross the small coffee house room?

I took it back to my table, thumping myself on the forehead for not rushing after. The words on the front "For you" filtering through me a dozen upon a dozen times. Unable to fight off a moment of curiosity, I relented to the excitement in my veins, that pumped to my fingers, and I opened the small book. But it was not a thing written for me while sitting in Morning Joe. It

## THE WORDS OF ANOTHER

was a work of time and patience. Letters and words filled the pages and I understood that this could not be - *for me*. It was from another, and it was for another. It was an empty thing at one time. Perhaps it was a gift, *for you*, it said. And then it was filled one page at a time by the one who was driving away.

Yes, so there it was, a gift, now filled. There it was in my hands, which have probably never held so much. It was special. I would come back for such a thing, surely anybody would. Ordering another drink, I waited, tapping the book, shifting it idly.

Old faces, new faces, wafting aromas, and eventually - the setting sun. There it was still, left behind. Again I leafed through the pages, full to the edges, and allowed my eyes this time to catch up some words. Then to read a sentence. And my eyes could not stop reading. My words, or ones like them, were there before me in those pages. My own perceptions of life and sharing life were there. And I could no longer hold back my interest.

# FROM THE HEART

Thoughts. Ideas. Dreams. It all seemed so pure, as if a fine filter had sifted all things in life. There was clarity and inspiration there. Something in my mind, a switch, flipped. I read there in the fading light until the shop closed. I read beneath the tree until the sun was gone. I read on the sofa until sleep took me. I dreamed of the breeze, rocking me, and I dreamed of the stars, and their infinite wonder.

When I woke in the morning the world was calling me from the farthest corners, that are often overlooked, like the cramped and dark spaces in a cellar. I thought of a map in various shades of green to brown, hanging on a wall, with red pins and blue pins marking sporadic achievements. I bought a new home for my words, an ordinary notebook, and held the hope to make it extraordinary. I took to the back roads that went on for long stretches, sometimes following the sun, sometimes the clouds, and sometimes nothing at all. The gas tank emptied, and the pages filled. I stopped whenever I heard my name being called from the sky, from the hills, or from nothing at all…

Down roads winding like an ancient river, past marshes and forests, twisting up and down mountains, I drove, getting out on my own feet as often as possible. I could have collected the wild flowers I found, gathered the fallen feathers of every bird, and snapped photos of the amazing things the sun can do at the beginning and end of each day. In a way, I did. In my way, it was all recorded. I rarely knew where I was, and fewer times did it matter. All I had known of the world and seen in it, a seemingly endless array of color and beauty, proved to be less than a fraction of the truth.

Countless people crossed paths with me. Each of us at a different step of the same journey. Cameras, easels, backpacks, and hearts full to the brim. I learned that the magnificence of the world was in its people, their wonder unlocked with a simple smile. Each one a being of hope and thought, lying beneath a thin layer, like an egg shell.

But there was sadness and worry in the world, too. Those things that many combated with their travels and with the taking in of the life around them. The thin protective layers we all wore cracked a little bit each day between the journey and the companionship. Everything I encountered etched itself deep inside my mind. In the end, a thing came to me:

> To share the world as I felt it would be little, if not nothing. Despite all my wanting of it.

> But to teach another how to feel the world on their own terms, that would be everything.

The pages were near to full, save the last one. Afterward would be the inevitable return home. A hollowness in my stomach won over the emptiness of the gas tank, and guided me to a small diner serving "The County's Best" coffee. It seemed a fitting book end to my days of traveling.

The server brought me a cup, steaming in the cool air. I sat in a booth, in the sunlight, and it was marvelous. My book was opened to the last page, which stared at me expectantly. Perhaps endings are harder to write than beginnings. We gazed at each other a long time, that page and I. We sat in the silence of old friends who have shared everything and don't know what else to talk about. Drinking good coffee, with pen in hand awaiting, and nothing to say.

A server stood in the corner, between the occasional request for ketchup and the freshening of mugs of coffee. I watched as words were scrawled onto a small notepad used for taking orders. A page was torn off, and put safely in a pocket. I couldn't help but half grin as I looked on, and surprisingly I didn't turn away when our eyes met. A sense of oneness existed there, like a secret handshake known only to those who *see*.

I looked to the people in their booths for the last inspiration. They were all probably old faces here. I was the new face. The bell rang, another presumably old face walked in, and in my mind I swear heard a "Mornin' Joe!"

Beginnings and ends. That's what the last

page would be. Like a Hawaiian "Aloha." My pen moved without hesitation and filled the last four corners, amidst small pauses for fantastic coffee, until at last, the white of the page was spent. I closed the ordinary looking notebook, set down my pen, and drank the last.

Collecting my things, I stood up and went to pay the cashier. "What did you think of 'The County's Best'?" She took the change from my hand and dropped it into the register.

"I swear by all the tea in China, it was the best coffee I've ever had." And it was. I noticed her name tag and couldn't help but smile; of course, it wouldn't be any other way. Beginnings and ends, I thought.

The server still stood in the corner, looking on at customers, writing down a new thought. I did the obvious thing, the only thing left to do before going home. I took out my pen, and on the front of my ordinary notebook, wrote the words "For you." I set it down on the table next to my empty mug, and walked to the door.

# THE WORDS OF ANOTHER

The bell rang when I opened the door, and the cashier waved. I turned to her and said, "Have a Good Morning, Jo."

# ABOUT THE AUTHOR
# - ABOUT ME -

Hi. I'm Jamie. But, you already knew that.

I'm a dreamer. I like to dream. In comfy chairs at home, in coffee shops, with my eyes closed and my mind open. I like to write about the people that I see in those dreams, they inspire me and make me wonder, make me think. They are, I think, a part of something bigger.

I am optimistic. I like to hope. And I like to write about that hope, and about faith, and about happiness. If these things are somehow relayed in these stories – then I am happy. If these things are somehow instilled in your own self in some way – then I am thrilled, and I am honored to be a part of that for you

I am also flawed. Just like my characters. I am finished, but not perfect. Just like my stories. Aren't we all? Isn't the beautiful thing that we can just keep becoming more every day? Passing these stories on, with the dream and hope that they will find the hands of those that need them, it's a step for me in becoming more.

Thank you for being a part of that for me.

Made in the USA
San Bernardino, CA
14 March 2017